Thomas and Lady Hatt's Birthday Party

**Based on *The Railway Series*
by The Rev. W. Awdry**

EGMONT

Bertie dropped some passengers off at the station.
"Have you noticed something strange today?"
he asked Thomas and Percy.
"What sort of something?" asked Thomas.
"The Fat Controller is acting rather strangely,"
replied Bertie.
"I saw him staring at the sky earlier," said Percy.
"I did wonder what he was thinking about."
The reason was simple. It was Lady Hatt's birthday
and Sir Topham Hatt, The Fat Controller, was
thinking about his new suit that he was going to
wear to Lady Hatt's party that afternoon.

"Your new suit will be perfect for my party," said Lady Hatt to her husband, The Fat Controller. "Thank you! I'll wear my finest hat, too," said The Fat Controller. "After all, your birthday is a very special occasion!"

"Don't be late, will you?" said Lady Hatt. "My party starts at three o'clock!"

"I'm working at another station today," replied The Fat Controller. "But don't worry, I'll do my very best to be right on time."

Thomas was working very hard on his branch line. He was moving heavy trucks loaded with rocks. His Fireman was busy, too. He was shovelling coal into the furnace to help Thomas work quickly.

"Phew!" said Thomas' Fireman, wiping his hand across his hot face. "This is very hard work on this hot day!"

Thomas agreed. It was hard work, but it made him feel like a Really Useful Engine!

The Fat Controller was working at another station that day. At two o'clock, he changed into his new yellow waistcoat and black suit, so he was ready for Lady Hatt's birthday party.

"You look fine, Sir!" said the Station Master. "But you'd best be going now," he added, looking at his watch.

"Indeed!" said The Fat Controller. "As the engines are busy working, I'll drive my car to the party."

The Fat Controller set off in the car to his station. He had only driven a little way down the road when he realised his car had a flat tyre. "Bother!" he said crossly, as he looked at the damaged wheel. "If I change the tyre myself, I will get my new suit dirty and that will never do!" He was just wondering what he could do instead, when Caroline the Car drove up.

"Hello, Caroline," said The Fat Controller. "My car has a flat tyre. Could you please give me a lift to my wife's birthday party?"

"Of course," said Caroline. "I would be happy to take you to Lady Hatt's party."

The Fat Controller asked Caroline to drive rather quickly. He was worried that he would arrive late for the party. Poor Caroline began to feel unwell. Before long, with steam pouring from her bonnet, she came to a sudden stop.

"Bother! Bother!" said The Fat Controller, "What am I going to do now?"

Just then, The Fat Controller heard a whistle. He turned round and saw George the Steamroller rolling down the road towards him.

"Can I help you, Sir?" asked George's Driver.

"Can you take me to my wife's birthday party, please?" asked The Fat Controller.

"Well, we can take you to Thomas," said George's Driver. "We saw him working further along the line. I'm sure Thomas will be able to take you straight to your station!"

"But, what about me?" wailed Caroline the Car, who was still feeling a little poorly.

"Don't worry, Caroline," said The Fat Controller. "When I get back to the station, I'll send someone to help you and repair my car, too. You wait right there, Caroline!" he added.

"That's all I can do!" coughed Caroline, as she watched The Fat Controller climb aboard the steamroller. George then rolled away, taking The Fat Controller to Thomas.

Oh, dear! The Fat Controller's new suit and hat were being splashed with George's dirty engine oil! But worse was to come. Just as George reached Thomas, his brakes failed and he lost control! He rolled right across the road and fell into a muddy ditch. The Fat Controller was sent flying through the air and landed up to his waist in the mud!

"Bother! Bother! BOTHER!" cried The Fat Controller, crossly.

Thomas and his Driver were shocked to see The Fat Controller covered in mud.

"Can we help you, Sir?" asked Thomas' Driver.

"Yes, please!" replied The Fat Controller, as he climbed out of the ditch. "Can you take me back to the station as fast as possible? I don't want to be late for my wife's birthday party, which starts at three o'clock."

"I'm afraid our Fireman is not feeling well," said Thomas' Driver. "He has been working very hard in this hot weather and now he needs a rest. We can't move unless someone does his job."

"It's not a problem, I'll do it!" said The Fat Controller. Thomas was very proud to have such a special Fireman. The Fat Controller got rather hot and dirty keeping Thomas' furnace stoked with coal. He was covered in coal dust too, but he didn't mind at all because he knew Thomas would get him to the station as fast as he could.

Thomas reached the station just after three o'clock. "Thank you!" said The Fat Controller to Thomas, his Driver and his tired Fireman. "You have all done a hard day's work. You can finish now and go and have a good rest!"
The Fat Controller looked up at the station clock. Seeing he was a little late, he rushed over to the flower stall and bought a large bunch of flowers for Lady Hatt.

The Fat Controller, in his now dirty and damaged new suit, rushed through the station with the flowers. When he reached the party, no one could see him, they could only see the large bunch of flowers he was hiding behind! As he walked into the room, everyone was shocked to see his muddy and oily clothes. The Fat Controller smiled at Lady Hatt. He knew he was dirty and a little late, but he had done his very best to get there on time, so he had kept his promise to her.

"Thank you, my dear!" said Lady Hatt, as The Fat Controller gave her the lovely bunch of flowers. She looked in surprise at his muddy and oily jacket and his torn and stained trousers.

"I know this is my party," she said with a smile, "but I didn't realise it was a fancy dress party!" Everyone, including The Fat Controller, laughed loudly and Lady Hatt's birthday party began.

First published in Great Britain 2002
by Egmont Books Limited
239 Kensington High Street, London W8 6SA
Story adapted from *Lady Hatt's Birthday Party*.
Photographs © Gullane (Thomas) Ltd. 1998.
All Rights Reserved.

Thomas the Tank Engine & Friends

A BRITT ALLCROFT COMPANY PRODUCTION

Based on The Railway Series by The Rev W Awdry

© Gullane (Thomas) Limited 2002

ISBN 1 4052 0120 7
1 3 5 7 9 10 8 6 4 2
Printed in Great Britain.